Joseph Robertson

An essay on culinary poisons

Joseph Robertson

An essay on culinary poisons

ISBN/EAN: 9783741176203

Manufactured in Europe, USA, Canada, Australia, Japa

Cover: Foto ©Andreas Hilbeck / pixelio.de

Manufactured and distributed by brebook publishing software
(www.brebook.com)

Joseph Robertson

An essay on culinary poisons

A N
E S S A Y
O N
CULINARY POISONS.

C O N T A I N I N G

C A U T I O N S

RELATIVE TO THE

USE of LAUREL-LEAVES,

HEMLOCK, MUSHROOMS, COPPER-VESSELS,
EARTHEN JARS, &c.

W I T H

Obfervations on the ADULTERATION of BREAD
and FLOUR,

And the NATURE and PROPERTIES of WATER.

Unde fames homini vetitorum tanta ciborum ?
Audetis vefci, genus ô mortale ? quod, oro,
Ne facite ; et monitis animos advertite noftris.

OVID. MET. xv. 138.

L O N D O N.
Printed for G. KEARSLY, at No. 46, near Serjeants
Inn, Fleet-Street,

M,DCC,LXXXI.

CONTENTS.

P R E-

PREFACE.

MANKIND are fubject to innumerable difeafes, from which
other animals are exempted. But
from whence do thefe difeafes arife?
From the feeds of mortality in the
human frame? From luxury and in-
temperance? Or from an indifcreet
ufe of vegetable and mineral poifons in the preparation of our food?
---From the laft of thefe fources we
certainly derive many troublefome,
and fometimes fatal diforders: fo
that, on many occafions, we may
exclaim with the fons of the pro-
phets*, " There is death in the
pot!"

* 2 Kings iv. 40.

The

The defign of this publication is to guard people againft thefe difaf-ters ; and, if poffible, to prevent fome of the calamities of human life. If it fhould anfwer this ufefu? purpofe, the author's ambition will be fully gratified.

CULINARY POISONS.

1. The LAURO-CERASUS, or Common LAUREL.

THE water diftilled from the leaves of this tree has been frequently mixed with brandy, and other fpirituous liquors, in order to give them the flavour of ratifia; and the leaves are often ufed in cookery, to communicate the fame kind of tafte to cream, cuftards, puddings, and fome forts of fweetmeats. But, in the year 1728, an account of two women dying fuddenly in Dublin, after drinking fome of the common diftilled laurel water, gave rife to feveral experiments, made upon dogs, with the diftilled water, and with the infufion of the leaves of the

B   lauro-

lauro-cerafus, communicated by Dr. Madden, phyfician at Dublin, to the Royal Society in England, and afterwards repeated (in the year 1731) and confirmed by Dr. Mortimer, F. R. S. by which it appeared, that both the water and the infufion brought on convulfions, palfy, and death, when taken by the mouth, or anus *.

Dr. Mead † fpeaks of the foregoing accident and experiments in thefe terms : " A fmall quantity of this water killed two women, who drank it, very fuddenly. Hereupon a learned phyfician, furprized at the event, (this plant having never been thought to be any wife noxious) made feveral experiments with it upon dogs, which were afterwards, fome of them, repeated here, with the fame fatal fuccefs."

Dr. Mortimer affirms, " that laurel-water is equally mortal with the bite of the rattle-fnake, and more quick in its operations than any mineral poifon."

* See Philofophical Tranfactions, No. 418, and 420.

† Mead on Poifons, Effay v.

Dr.

Dr. James fays: "laurel-water is the moft deleterious poifon perhaps known, killing almoft inftantaneoufly ‡."

The laurus of the ancients, or the *bay*, is, on the contrary, of a falutary nature, and of ufe in feveral diforders.

It may be faid, that the laurel in cuftards, and other articles of cookery, is ufed in very fmall quantities, and has never been attended with any pernicious effect.——But, I afk, who can pretend to affert, that it has not occafioned fome latent diforder, or fome complaints, which have been afcribed to other caufes? What perfon of fenfe or prudence would truft to the difcretion of an ignorant cook, in the ufe of a dangerous ingredient in his puddings or cuftards? Or, who, but a madman, would choofe to feafon his victuals with poifon?

The remedy is from ten to forty drops of fal ammoniac, in a glafs of water, repeated as the fymptoms may require.

‡ James's Difpenfatory, book iii. c. 1. p. 228.

2. Small

2. Small HEMLOCK, or FOOL'S PARSLEY.

DESCRIPTION.

The firſt leaves are divided into numerous ſmall parts, which are of a pale green, oval, pointed, and deeply indented. The ſtalk is ſlender, round, upright, ſtriated, and about a yard high. The flowers are white, growing at the tops of the branches in little umbells. It is an annual plant, common in orchards and kitchen gardens, and flowers in June and July. This plant has been often miſtaken for parſley: and from thence it has received the name of *Fools Parſley*.

Though it ſeems not to be of ſo virulent a nature as the larger hemlock, yet Boerhaave places it among the vegetable poiſons, in his Inſtitutes; and, in his Hiſtory of Plants, produces an inſtance of its pernicious effects ‡. It is therefore

‡ Inſtitutes, § 1138, Hiſt. of Plants, p. 93.

fore neceſſary to guard againſt it in collecting
herbs for ſallads, and other purpoſes.

---

3. MUSHROOMS.

Muſhrooms have been long uſed in ſauces, in
ketchup, and other forms of cookery. They were
highly eſteemed by the Romans, as they are at
preſent, by the French, Italians, and other na-
tions.

Pliny exclaims againſt the luxury of his coun-
trymen in this article ; and wonders, what extra-
ordinary pleaſure there can be, in eating ſuch *dangerous food**. The ancient writers on the Materia
Medica ſeem to agree, that muſhrooms are in general unwholeſome ; and the moderns, Lemery,
Allen, Geoffroy, Boerhaave, Linnæus, and others,
concur in the ſame opinion. There are numerous inſtances upon record of their fatal effects.
Al-

---

* Quæ voluptas tanta *ancipitis* cibi ?   Plin. Nat. Hiſt.
x xii, 23.

Almoſt all of them, as the laſt-mentioned author affirms, " are fraught with poiſon †."

The common eſculent kinds, if eaten too freely, frequently bring on heart-burns, ſickneſſes, vomitings, diarrhœas, dyſenteries, and other dangerous ſymptoms. It is therefore to be wiſhed, that they were baniſhed from the table. But, if the palate muſt be indulged in theſe treacherous gratifications, or, as Seneca ‡ calls them, this " voluptuous poiſon", it is neceſſary, that they, who are employed in collecting them, ſhould be extremely cautious, left they ſhould collect ſuch as are abſolutely pernicious; which, conſidering to whoſe care this is generally committed, may, and undoubtedly has, frequently happened §.

† Fungi plerique VENENO TURGENT. Linnæi Amœn. Acad. vol. 1.

‡ Quid tu illos boletos, VOLUPTARIUM VENENUM, nihil occulti operis judicas facere, etiamſi præſentanei non furant? SEN. EP. 95.

§ See Gentleman's Magazine, December, 1755; and Supplement, September, 1757.

The

The eatable mushrooms at first appear of a roundish form, like a button ; the upper part and the stalk are very white ; the under part is of a livid flesh-colour ; but the fleshy part, when broken, is very white. When these are suffered to remain undisturbed, they will grow to a large size, and expand themselves almost to a flatness, and the red part underneath will change to a dark colour.

COPPER VESSELS.

Copper, when it is handled, yields an offensive smell, and if touched with the tongue, a sharp pungent taste, and even excites a nausea. Verdegris is nothing but a solution of this metal by vegetable acids. And it is well known, that a very small quantity of this solution will produce cholics, vomitings, intolerable thirst, universal con-

convulfions, and other dangerous fymptoms. If thefe effects, and the prodigious divifibility of this metal be confidered, there can be no doubt of its being a violent and fubtile poifon, We are daily expofed to this poifon by the prefent ufe of copper veffels for dreffing our food. The very air of the kitchen, abounding with oleaginous and faline particles, penetrates and difpofes them to diffolution, before they are ufed. Water, by ftanding fome time in a copper veffel, is impregnated with verdegris, as may be demonftrated by throwing into it a fmall quantity of any volatile alkali, which will immediately tinge it with a paler or deeper blue, in proportion to the ruft contained in the water. Vinegar, apple-fauce, greens, oil, greafe, butter, and almoft every other kind of food, will extract the verdegris in a greater degree. It is true, people imagine, that the ill effects of copper are prevented by its being tinned : but the tin, which adheres to the copper, is fo extremely thin, that it is foon penetrated by the verdegris, which infinuates itfelf through the pores of that metal, and appears green upon the furface.

M. Amy,

M. Amy, of the Academy of Sciences at Paris, obferves, that " verdegris is one of the moft violent poifons in nature :" yet, fays he, " rather than quit an old cuftom, the greater part of mankind are content to fwallow fome of this poifon every day". Amy's Treat. upon Cifterns, printed at Paris, 1750.

M. Thiery, in a thefis, which is added to this tract, has more particularly confidered the noxious qualities of copper, and the various means, by which they may be communicated to whatever we eat or drink. " Our food, fays he, receives its quantity of poifon in the kitchen, by the ufe of copper pans and difhes. The brewer mingles poifon in our beer, by boiling it in a copper. Salt is diftributed to the people from copper fcales, covered with verdegris." Pickled cucumbers are rendered green by an infufion of copper coin. " The paftry-cook bakes our tarts in copper patty-pans. But confections and fyrups have greater powers of deftruction : for they are fet over a fire in copper veffels, which have not been tinned; and the verdegris is plentifully extracted by the acidity of the compofition. And though we do not, after all, fwallow

C   death

death in a single dose, yet it is certain, that a quantity of poison, however small, which is repeated with every meal, must produce more fatal effects, than is generally believed".

Bell-metal kettles are very often used in boiling cucumbers for pickling, in order to make them green. This is an absurd and dangerous practice. If the cucumbers acquire any additional greenness by the use of these kettles, they can only derive it from the copper, of which they are made.

According to some writers, bell-metal is a composition of tin and copper, or pewter and copper, in the proportion of twenty pounds of pewter, or twenty-three pounds of tin, to one hundred weight of copper. According to others, this metal is made of copper, a thousand pounds; tin, from two to three hundred pounds; and brass, one hundred and fifty pounds *.

Spoons and other kitchen utensils are frequently made of a mixed metal, called alchemy; or, as it is vulgarly pronounced, ockimy. The rust of this metal, as well as the former, is highly pernicious.

* Lord Bacon's Phyf. Remains.

White

White alchemy is made of pan-brafs, one pound; and arfenicum, three ounces. Red alchemy is made of copper, and auripigmentum, or orpiment †.

The author of a tract, entitled, Serious Reflections on the dangers attending the ufe of copper veffels, publifhed at London in 1755, afferts, that " the greater frequency of palfies, apoplexies, madnefs, and all the frightful train of nervous diforders, which fuddenly attack us, without our being able to account for the caufe, or which gradually weaken our vital faculties, are the poifonous effects of this pernicious matter, taken into the body infenfibly with our victuals, and thereby intermixed with our blood and juices".

However this may be, it is certain, that there have been innumerable inftances of the pernicious confequences of eating food dreffed in copper veffels, not fufficiently cleaned from this ruft. On this account the Senate of Sweden, about the year 1753, prohibited copper veffels, and ordered, that none, but fuch as were made of iron, fhould be ufed in their fleets and armies.

† Lord Bacon's Phyf. Remains.

But

But if copper veffels are ftill continued, every cook and good houfewife fhould be particularly careful in keeping them clean and well tinned; and fhould fuffer nothing to remain in them longer, than it is abfolutely neceffary for the purpofe of cookery.

REMEDY.

" The common cure, fays Dr. Mead, of all poifons taken into the ftomach, muft be by throwing them up again, by vomiting, as foon as poffible, and defending the membranes from their pungent acrimony. Drinking very large quantities of warm milk, with oil of fweet almonds, till the vomiting ceafes, will anfwer the firft intention. The other, in mineral poifons, (for the effects of vegetable poifons, after they have been vomited up, generally go off by diluting plentifully with foft and fat liquids) requires particular care, which may be in this way. The force of thefe depends upon a combination of metallic particles with faline cryftals: therefore the difuniting of thefe muft deftroy their power. This

may.

may be done by drinking a quantity of a lixivium made by a solution of salt of tartar in water : for this salt, uniting with the corrosive cryftalline salt, will, after fome degree of effervefcence, kill it, as the chemifts fpeak ; by which means, being difengaged from the mineral globules, it will be rendered of no effect"*.

●

The SOLUTION or SALT of LEAD.

Lead is a metal eafily corroded, efpecially by the warm fteams of acids, fuch as vinegar, cyder, lemon-juice, rhenifh wine, &c. And this folution, or falt of lead, is a flow and infidious, though certain poifon. The glazing of all our common brown pottery ware, is either lead or lead ore. If black, it is lead ore, with a fmall proportion of manganefe, which is a fpecies of iron ore. If yellow, the glazing is lead ore, and appears yellowifh by having fome pipe or white clay

* Mead on Poifons, Effay iv.

clay under it. The colour of the common pottery ware is red, as the veffels are made of the fame clay with common bricks. Thefe veffels are fo porous, that they are penetrated by all falts, acid or alkaline, and are unfit for retaining any faline fubftance. They are improper, though too often ufed, for preferving four fruits or pickles. The glazing of fuch veffels is corroded by the vinegar; for, upon evaporating the liquor, a quantity of the falt of lead will be found at the bottom. A fure way of judging, whether the vinegar, or other acids, have diffolved part of the glazing, is, by their becoming vapid, or lofing their fharpnefs, and acquiring a fweetifh tafte by ftanding in them for fome time : in which cafe the contents are to be thrown away as pernicious.

The fubftance of the pottery ware commonly called Delft, the beft being made at Delft in Holland, is a whitifh clay when baked, and foft, as not having endured a great heat in baking. The glazing is a compofition of calcined lead, calcined tin, fand, fome coarfe alkaline falt, and fandiver ; which being run into a white glafs, the white colour being owing to the tin, is afterwards
ground

ground in a mill, then mixed with water, and the veffels, after being baked in the furnace, are dipped into it, and put into the furnace a fecond time ; by which means, with a fmall degree of heat, the white glafs runs upon the veffels. This glazing is exceedingly foft and eafily cracks. What effects acids will have upon it, the author of thefe obfervations cannot fay, not having tried them : but they feem to be improper for infpiffating the juice of lemons, oranges, or any other acid fruits.

The moft proper veffels for thefe purpofes are porcelain or china ware. The fubftance of them is of fo clofe a texture, that no faline, or other liquor, can penetrate them. The glazing, which is made likewife of the fubftance of the china, is fo firm and clofe, that no falt or faline fubftance can have the leaft effect upon it. It muft, however, be obferved, that this remark is only applicable to the porcelain made in China : for fome fpecies of the European manufactory are certainly glazed with a fine glafs of lead, &c.

Next to china is the ftone ware, commonly called the Staffordfhire ware. The fubftance of thefe

thefe veffels is a compofition of black flint, and a
ftrong clay, that bakes white. Their outfides
are glazed by throwing into the furnace, when
well heated, common or fea falt decrepitated ;
the fteam or acid of which, flying up among the
veffels, vitrifies the outfides of them, and gives
them the glazing. This ftone ware does not appear to be injured or affected by any kind of falts,
either acid or alkaline, or any liquors, hot or
cold. They are therefore extremely proper for
all common ufes, but require a careful manage-
ment, as they are much apter to crack with any
fudden heat, than china.

The Heffian ware, or the veffels made of the
fame fubftance with the Duke d'Alva's bottles,
commonly called grey-beards, feem to be made of
ftrong pipe clay, mixed with fand, and glazed in
the baking, by the alkaline falt, which arifes from
the wood ufed in baking them, wood having always the effect, when the furnace is intenfe, to vi-
trify the outfide of all clays*.

* Differt. by James Lind, M. D.

REMARKS

REMARKS on the ADULTERATION of BREAD and FLOUR.

Extracted from a Treatise " On the nature of bread, honestly and dishonestly made", published in 1757, by JAMES MANNING, M. D.

———————

The author tells us, that in the sophistication of flour, mealmen and bakers have been known to use bean meal, chalk, whiting, slaked lime, alum, and even ashes of bones. The first, bean flour, is perfectly innocent, and affords a nourishment equal to that of wheat; but there is a toughness in bean flour, and its colour is dusky. To remove these defects, chalk is added to whiten it, alum to give the whole compound that consistence, which is necessary to make it knead well in the dough, and jalap to take off the astringency. It may be supposed, that these horrid iniquities are only imaginary, or at least exaggerated, and that such mixtures must

D

be

be difcoverable even by the moft ordinary tafte;
but as fome adulterations of this nature have certainly been practiced, the following experiments
may ferve to gratify curiofity, or difcover frauds,
where any fuch exift.

" To difcover whether flour be adulterated
with whiting or chalk, mix with it fome juice of
lemon or good vinegar. If the flour be pure,
they will remain together at reft ; but if there be
a mixture of whiting or chalk, a fermentation,
like the working of yeft, will enfue. The adulterated meal is whiter and heavier than the good :
the quantity that an ordinary tea-difh will contain, has been found to weigh more than the fame
quantity of genuine flour, by four drachms, and
19 grains, Troy.

" The regular method to detect thefe frauds`
in bread is this : cut the crum of a loaf into very
thin flices ; break them, but not into very fmall
pieces, and put them into a glafs cucurbit, with a
large quantity of water. Set this, without fhaking, in a fand furnace, and let it ftand, with a mo-
derate warmth, four and twenty hours. The
crumb of the bread will in this time foften in all

its

its parts, and the ingredients will feperate from it. The alum will diffolve in the water, and may be extracted from it in the ufual way. The jalap, if any have been ufed, will fwim upon the top in a coarfe film, and the other ingredients, being heavy, will fink to the bottom. This is the beft and moft regular method of finding the deceit ; but as cucurbits, and fand furnaces, are not at hand in private families, there is a more familiar method.

" Let the crum of a loaf be fliced as before directed, and put it, with a great deal of water, into a large earthen pipkin. Let this be fet over a very gentle fire, and kept a long time moderately hot ; and the pap being poured off, the bone afhes, or other ingredients, will be found at the bottom."

ON

On WATER.

Observations on Water, extracted from Dr. Rotherham's Philosophical Enquiry, &c.

IT is a long established observation, that the best waters boil and cool again the soonest; and that they evaporate in the least time, and with the least degree of heat.

A well known mark of the purity of water is its softness. This quality is discoverable by the touch, if we only wash our hands in it: and the distinction between hard and soft water generally arises from its difficult or easy union with oily substances,

Soft

Soft water is the moſt proper for the waſhing and bleaching of linen, the making of paper, and for moſt medicinal purpoſes. It mixes more uniformly with milk, and does not curdle it, as hard waters frequently do. It boils peaſe and beans ſofter, and mixes better with flour, rice, oatmeal, &c. In boiling meat it gives it a more agreeable colour than hard water, which often boils it red.

There are however ſome purpoſes, to which hard water is more proper : as, in ſeveral kinds of dying; in making ſtarch ; and in the rincing of ſoap out of linen, after it has been waſhed ; as it is obſerved to give the linen a better colour, and an agreeable firmneſs or criſpneſs ; but the linen thus treated requires more ſoap, when it comes to be waſhed again. Hard water gives a better colour to greens, and a firmneſs to all ſorts of fiſh, eſpecially cod, when boiled in it.

The Burton, Nottinghamſhire, Liverpool, and ſeveral other kinds of ale, which are much admired, are ſaid to be brewed with hard water. But Dr. Mead and others condemn the uſe of theſe liquors, as productive of various diſorders, and particularly the cholic.

From

From thefe remarks we may reafonably infer, that hard water cannot fo well anfwer the purpofes of diluting and digefting our food ; as it will not fo readily mix and unite with the different parts of it, nor affimulate and digeft them properly. Befides the large quantities of acid and nitrous falts, with the loads of felenite and calcareous earth, which thefe waters generally contain, will naturally difpofe them to form obftrudtions, when, by the courfe of circulation, thefe folid particles come into the minuteft veffels, more efpecially thofe of the glands. Hence they are often blamed, as laying the foundation of frophulous, ftrumous, and other glandular fwellings and obftrudtions.

It is from the quantity of ftony matter, which the hard waters generally contain, that moft of them have large incruftations upon the fides of the veffels, in which they are boiled; and they have by fome been difapproved for this reafon, as caufing the ftone. But the calculous concretions in the bladder and kidneys are of a very different nature from thefe incruftations ; and, as Dr. Heberden juftly obferves, " they totally differ from all foffil ftones in every thing except the name ; and the

pre-

pretended experience of the effects of certain ftony waters in breeding the ftone, may, upon the beft authorities, be rejected as falfe*.

The beft way of determing the hardnefs or foftnefs of water, is by fcraping any certain quantity of foap into it, and obferving how it diffolves or lathers. If water be perfectly foft, the foap will diffolve quickly, uniformly, and without curdling ; and, upon fhaking the glafs brifkly, will raife a ftrong froth or lather at the top. But the fmalleft degree of hardnefs will fhew itfelf, either by the foap not diffolving fo readily, by its turning curdly and uneven, or by lefs froth remaining after it is agitated ; and the different degrees of hardnefs may hereby be very well determined. The beft way of making this trial is with a fmall quantity of Caftile foap, viz. about a grain to an ounce of water.

RAIN-WATER.

In fummer-time rain-water brings along with it the feeds and embryos of vegetables and animalcula,

† Medical Tranf. by the Coll. of Phyf. vol. 1. p. 7.

malcua, which render it difagreeable to the tafte, and promote its putrefaction. If it be kept in wooden veffels, it will foon ftink, and become unfit for ufe; and then, if it be viewed with a microfcope, it will be found to contain an amazing number of various animalcula; and particularly thofe, which, from their form and motion, are called the wheel animals*. Thefe animalcula are fuppofed to be the chief caufe of the water's putrefaction.

Rain water is a little hard, when it firft falls; but in two or three days it becomes perfectly foft.

The rain, which falls through the fmoke of large towns, is rendered foul and black; more especially if it be collected, as it generally is, from the roofs of houfes; when it brings with it a great many particles of foot, which give it a very difagreeable tafte and colour. Where the tiles are blackened by the fmoke of glafs-houfes, &c. the water,

* Baker's Microfcope made eafy, p. 83. Employment for the Microfcope, p. 295.

water, which falls from them, is unfit for almoft any domeftic purpofes.

When rain-water fubfides, and is well filtered, it becomes perfectly clear and bright. If it be kept in wooden veffels, it contracts a particular fmell, tafte and colour from the wood.

Clean earthen jars are the beft for keeping water. Though leaden cifterns may be ufed with fafety, if they be kept clear from vegetable acids; all of which are found to corrode lead, and to produce a very noxious falt. The veffels, in which water is preferved, fhould be covered, to prevent any duft or filth from getting in; and the water will be more agreeable, if kept in a cool place.

SNOW - WATER.

Some of the greateft philofophers and phyficians have differed much in their opinion of fnow-water. Hippocrates, Hoffman, and others, condemn it. But Boerhaave, on the other hand, is

E · la-

lavifh in its encomiums. He afferts, that fnow, which is collected from the tops of high fandy mountains, at a diftance from any towns or houfes, where it has fallen after a long fharp froft, in calm weather, and lies at a confiderable height above the furface of the earth, produces water, " which is the pureft of all, quite immutable, capable of being kept for many years, and is a fingular remedy for inflammations of the eyes" *.

Dr. Rotheram having mentioned the efficacy of fnow-water in burns, and in fertilizing the ground, relates the following experiment, which, though it may appear of a trivial nature, he very juftly remarks, is not below the notice of a philofopher.

" One effect of fnow, of which I do not remember any where to have read, is, that a certain quantity of it, taken up frefh from the ground, and mixed in a flour-pudding, will fupply the place of eggs, and make it equally light. The quantity allotted is two table fpoonfuls, inftead of one egg ; and if this proportion be much exceeded, the pudding will not adhere together, but will fall to pieces in boiling. I affert this from the experience

* Boerh. Chem. vol. 1. p. 349. London edit. 1735.

rience of my own family; and any one, who choofes to try it, will find it to be a fact".

SPRING WATER.

As all our fprings are originally fupplied by rain, or melted fnow, and hail, ftrained through the pores and cavities of the earth, their waters will vary according to the different foils, or ftrata, through which they pafs. If waters meet with nothing in their fubterraneous paffages, which will unite with them, or diffolve in them, they iffue out in their greateft purity. The fprings, which come from gravel, fand, or fome light and porous ftones, are generally the pureft, and beft; for the water being filtered through their fmall pores, is cleared from almoft every foreign fubftance or impurity, which it had contracted in the air; acquires an agreeable coolnefs, and becomes limpid, bright, and fparkling.

But, as there are few foils, which do not contain fome kinds of falt, or other mineral fubftances, which are foluble in water, moft of our fprings are found to partake, in fome meafure, of

the

the nature of the foil, through which they pafs, and are innocent, falutary, or noxious, in proportion to the quantity, kind, or mixture, of the various ingredients, of which they are compofed ; and the conftitution, of the perfon, who ufes them : and fome of them are of great medicinal efficacy.

STAGNANT WATER.

Stagnant water in ponds and ditches is generally efteemed the worft. But large lakes, which are kept in almoft a continual agitation by the wind, do not properly come within the denomination of ftagnant waters.

PUMP WATER, efpecially in LONDON.

It appears from the analyfis performed by Dr. Heberden †, that feveral pump waters in London, which he had examined, and probably moft

of

---

† See Medical Tranfact. vol. 1.

of them, contain powder of lime-ftone, and the
mineral acids of vitriol, nitre, and fea-falt, united
in various proportions. Thefe waters are likewife tainted with an oilinefs, which gives them a
remarkably yellowifh caft, when compared with
pure diftilled water. It is reafonable to think,
that waters impregnated with fuch active fubftances, in a quantity fufficient to render them
difagreeable to the tafte, cannot always be drunk
with impunity. They have accordingly been fuf-
pected of occafioning pains in the ftomach and
bowels, glandular tumors and coftivenefs, where
the fimple lime-ftone prevails ; and diarrhœas,
where much of it is united with the folution of a-
cids ; and it is probable, that a continued ufe of
fuch water may be the caufe of many other diforders, efpecially to the infirm, and to children.
From whence it follows, that a change of place
may often be of as much ufe to weak perfons,
from the change of water, as of air.

Some obfcure notion of the unwholefomenefs
of pump water, induces many perfons to boil it,
and let it ftand to grow cold ; by which it
will indeed be made to part from moft of its un-
neutralized lime-ftone and felenite ; but at the
fame time it will become more ftrongly impregnated

nated with the faline matter, and therefore it will be worfe.

If a fmall quantity of falt of tartar were added to the water, it would readily precipitate both the loofe lime-ftone, and likewife that which is united to the acids. Ten or fifteen grains would generally be enough for a pint; but the exact proportion would readily be found, by continuing to add to it, by little and little, till it ceafed to occafion white clouds. This is an eafy way, not only of freeing the water from its lime-ftone, but alfo of changing the faline part into nitre and fal fylvii, both of which we know, by long experience, to be innocent.

But the beft way of avoiding the bad effects of pump water would be, not to make a conftant ufe of it; and in a place fo well fupplied with river water as London, there is very little neceffity to drink of the fprings, which in fo large a city, befides their natural contents, muft collect many additional impurities from cellars, burying-grounds, common-fewers, and many other offenfive places, with which they undoubtedly often com-

communicate ; fo that it is indeed a wonder, that we find this water at all tolerable *.

THAMES and NEW-RIVER WATER.

River waters partake of the properties of their fprings, and the channels, through which they run ; yet, in a wonderful manner, they foon free themfelves from their impurities. The motion of the current †, the abforption of the foil, the fun and rain, have each of them a confiderable fhare in this effect.

The Thames water, efpecially in the neighbourhood of London, is mixed with many impure ingredients. It is faid to become offenfive in feven or eight days, or fometimes fooner, if it be kept in unfeafoned cafks. In this ftate it generates a quantity of foul inflammable air, as may be feen by holding the flame of a candle to the bung-hole of a cafk when it is firft opened. But by

* See Medical Tranfact. vol. 1.

† The moft rapid rivers contain, cæteris paribus, the pureft water.

by this fermentation it foon purifies itfelf; and by opening the bung, it will often become fweet in twenty-four hours, and fooner, if it be poured from one veffel to another, or ventilated *.

METHODS, BY WHICH WATER MAY BE OBTAINED IN ITS GREATEST PURITY.

As it appears, that almoft all the water ufed in cookery is tainted with impure ingredients; rain water, with a great variety of volatile bodies, fuliginous particles, exhalations, invifible feeds, and infects; river, pond, and well water, with a mixture of foil and mud, decayed vegetables, and the fpawn of vermin, it will be very proper to purify it, before it is ufed for drinking, or any culinary purpofe. This may be done by various contrivances.

1. The water of the Thames, and that of the New River, are very often muddy, or tafte ftrongly of weeds and leaves. Dr. Heberden acknowledges, that the latter fault cannot eafily be re-

* Philof. Tranf. No. 127, 268. Boerh. Elem. of Chem. vol. 1. p. 333. Rotheram's Philof. Inquiry.

remedied ; but, he obferves, they would foon be
freed from their muddinefs, if kept fome time in
an open jar : and he is of opinion, that if the water given to very young children, were thus puri-
fied, it might prevent fome of their bowel-difor-
ders, and fo contribute a little to leffen that a-
mazing mortality among the children, which are
nurfed in London.

2. Rain water, when grown putrid, as Boerhaave
affures us, may be eafily rendered wholefome a-
gain, and may be drunk without being offenfive,
by only boiling it a few moments : for by this
expedient, the animals that are in it will be de-
ftroyed, and, with the reft of the impurities, will
fubfide to the bottom. If then, fays he, you
make it moderately acid, by adding to it a fmall
quantity of acid that is very ftrong, it will be fit
for ufe. This is found to be of excellent fervice
under the Equator, and between the Tropics,
where the waters putrify in a horrible manner,
and breed a multitude of infects, and yet muft be
drunk. For the fame reafon, a fmall quantity of
fpirit of vitriol, mixed with water, will prevent its
growing putrid, and breeding any animals, and,

F

at the fame time, preferve it wholefome and good *.

3. A common way of purifying water is by fil-tration. Water, which is filterated through por-ous ftones, is extremely clear and limpid; but fome writers have afferted, that it acquires a pe-trifying quality in its paffage, which, at length, may produce difagreeable effects ‡. However this may be, thefe ftones are too dear for common ufe.

Dr. Rotheram afferts, that one of the readieft and beft methods of filtering water, is, to let it run through a bed of clean fand. This is, he fays, preferable to the filtering-ftone, as it per-forms its work much fooner; and the grains of fand are of fo many different figures, that they are pretty fure to ftop the progrefs of any bodies of fenfible bulk, in paffing through them §.

* Boerh. Chem. vol. 1. p. 348.

‡ M. Amy on Cifterns; but fee above, p. 31.

§ If you view ten thoufand grains of fand through a mi-crofcope, you will fcarcely find two of the fame fize and fhape. Rotheram's Philofophical Inquiry, p. 48.

" A friend

" A friend of mine, fays the Doctor, in this town [Newcaftle] has a ciftern for collecting rain water, fo conftructed, that it both allows the water to fubfide, and the upper part of it to run through a bed of fand, which is raifed by a partition above the bottom of the ciftern; by which means the water becomes perfectly clear and bright, and is preferred by moft who have tafted it, to any other water in this town".

4. Some have objected, but probably without reafon, to this mode of filtration, on a prefumption, that the fand has the fame effect on the water as the filtering ftone : for it is faid, that the fand is infenfibly diffolved by the water ; fo that in four or five years it will have loft a fifth part of its weight. M. Amy therefore recommends the filtration of water through a fpunge, more or lefs compreffed. And this, he affures us, will render it, not only more clear, but more wholefome, than either a ftone or fand.

5. As the pureft of all water is obtained by diftillation, Dr. Heberden recommends this method, as particularly ufeful where fuel is cheap,

F 2   and

and the water is bad ; as it is in some of our foreign settlements.

The first running of distilled water has a disagreeable musty taste: on this account, if the still hold twenty gallons, it will be necessary to throw away the first gallon. The rest, through free from this mustiness, will have a disagreeable empyreumatic or burnt taste. This taste goes off by keeping about a month, by ventillation, in a few minutes, or by boiling the water in an open vessel. Distilled water must be kept in perfectly clean glass or stone bottles, with glass stoppers, or metal covers; and then, having in it no principle of corruption, it is incapable of being spoiled, and will keep just the same for ever. But the least particle of any animal or vegetable substance, will spoil a great quantity ; and therefore the still and bottles should be kept wholly for this use.

This process, though certainly attended with many good effects, requires too much time and attention for common use; and therefore, in general, it may be sufficient to adopt the mode

of

of filteration, recommended by Dr. Rotheram, or that which is propofed by M. Amy.

The obfervations, which I have here laid before the reader, are not new. They have been communicated to the public by others. But they are difperfed through many different publications. I have therefore thrown them into a fmall compafs. And I flatter myfelf, that, in this commodious form, they may be acceptable to the public; as many of the foregoing articles are of infinite importance to the health, and confequently to the happinefs of mankind.

F I N I S.